To access the read-along audio, visit
WWW.HMHBOOKS.COM/FREEDOWNLOADS
ACCESS CODE: READGOSSIEANDFRIENDS

Gossie
wears bright
red boots.

Gertie
is Gossie's best
friend.

Ollie
likes to get
his way.

Gideon
does not like
to nap!

Peedie
sometimes
forgets things.

BooBoo
enjoys eating
"good food."

Jasper
likes to
be tidy.

Joop
likes to
be messy.

Gossie & Friends®

BIG BOOK of ADVENTURES

Olivier Dunrea

HOUGHTON MIFFLIN HARCOURT
Boston   New York

CONTENTS

Gossie

AGES	GRADES	GUIDED READING LEVEL	READING RECOVERY LEVEL	LEXILE® LEVEL
4–6	1	D	5–6	0

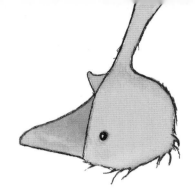

This is Gossie.
Gossie is a gosling.

A small, yellow gosling who
likes to wear bright red boots.

Every day.

She wears them
when she eats.

She wears them
when she sleeps.

She wears them when
she rides.

She wears them when
she hides.

But what Gossie *really* loves
is to wear her bright red boots
when she goes for walks.

Every day.

She walks backward.

She walks forward.

She walks uphill.

She walks downhill.

She walks in the rain.

She walks in the snow.

Gossie loves to wear
her bright red boots!

Every day.

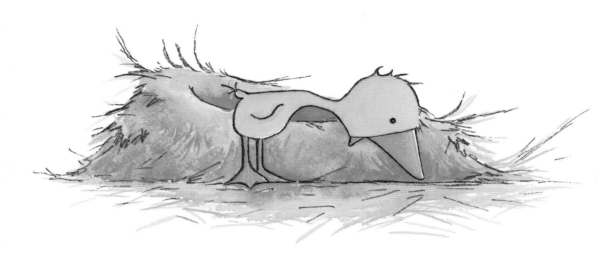

One morning Gossie could
not find her bright red boots.

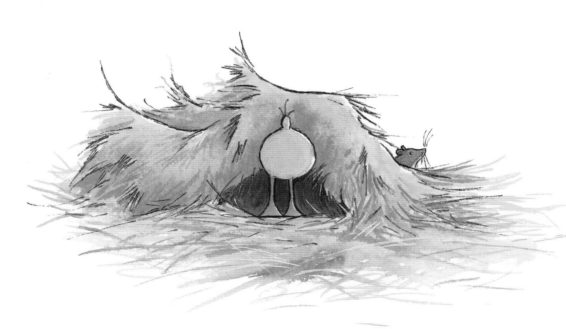

She looked everywhere.
Under the bed.

Over the wall.

In the barn.

Under the hens.

Gossie looked and looked
for her bright red boots.

They were gone.
Gossie was heartbroken.

Then she saw them.

They were walking.

On someone else's feet!

"Great boots!" said Gertie.
Gossie smiled.

Gossie is a gosling.
A small, yellow gosling who
likes to wear bright red boots.

Almost every day.

Gossie&Gertie

AGES	GRADES	GUIDED READING LEVEL	READING RECOVERY LEVEL	LEXILE® LEVEL
4–6	1	E	7–8	10L

This is Gossie.

This is Gertie.

Gossie wears bright red boots.
Gertie wears bright blue boots.

They are friends.
Best friends.

They splash in the rain.

They play hide-and-seek
in the daisies.

They dive in the pond.

They watch in the night.

They play in the haystacks.

Gossie and Gertie are
best friends.

Everywhere Gossie goes,

Gertie goes too.

"Follow me!" cried Gossie.
Gossie marched to the barn.

Gertie followed.

"Follow me!" cried Gossie.
Gossie sneaked to the sheep.

Gertie followed.

"Follow me!"
cried Gossie.

Gossie jumped
into a mud puddle.
Gertie did not follow.

"Follow me!"
shouted Gossie.

Gertie followed a
hopping frog.

"Follow me!"
shouted Gossie.

But Gertie followed
a butterfly.

"Follow me!"
shouted Gossie.

But Gertie followed
a shiny blue beetle.

"Follow me!" shouted Gossie
as she followed Gertie.

Gertie followed a trail
of grain.

"Follow me!" said Gertie.
"It's dinnertime."

Gossie followed.

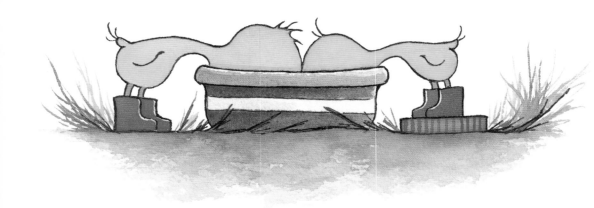

Gossie and Gertie are friends.
Best friends.

Ollie

AGES	GRADES	GUIDED READING LEVEL	READING RECOVERY LEVEL	LEXILE® LEVEL
4–6	1	F	9–10	30L

This is Ollie.

Ollie is waiting.

He won't come out.

Gossie and Gertie have been
waiting for weeks for Ollie
to come out.

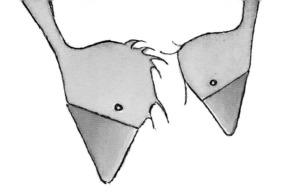

"I won't come out," says Ollie.

He rolls to the left.

He rolls to the right.

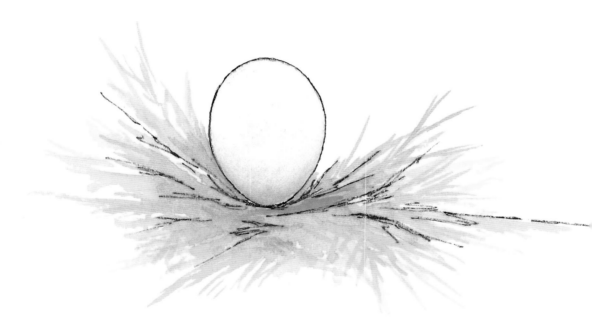

He stands on his head.

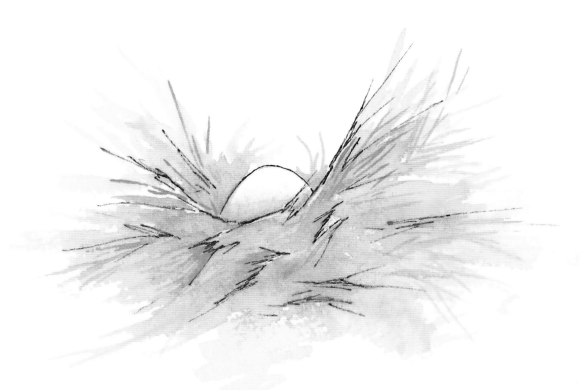

He hides in the straw.
He won't come out.

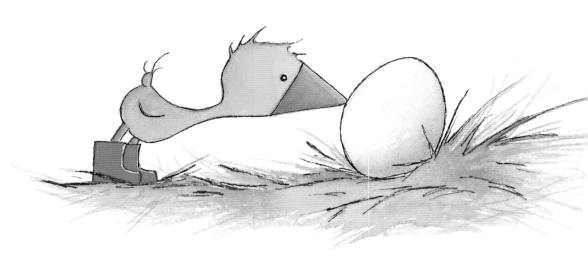

Gossie pokes Ollie with
her bill.

Gertie listens to Ollie with her ear.

"I won't come out!" says Ollie.

He holds his breath.

He rolls out of the nest.

He rolls over the stones.

He rolls under the sheep.
He won't come out.

Gossie runs after Ollie.

Gertie runs after Ollie.

"I won't come out!" says Ollie.

Gossie and Gertie sit on top
of Ollie.

"Don't come out," says Gossie.

"Don't come out," says Gertie.

Ollie waits.

Then he begins cracking!

"I'm out!" he says.

Ollie the Stomper

AGES	GRADES	GUIDED READING LEVEL	READING RECOVERY LEVEL	LEXILE® LEVEL
4–6	1	E	7–8	270L

This is Ollie.

This is Gossie. This is Gertie.

They are goslings.

Gossie wears bright red boots.

Gertie wears bright blue boots.

Ollie wants boots.

Gossie and Gertie tromp
in the straw.

Ollie stomps after them.

Gossie and Gertie romp
in the rain.

Ollie stomps after them.

Gossie and Gertie jump
over a puddle.

Ollie stomps after them.

Gossie and Gertie march
to the pond.

Ollie stomps after them.

Gossie and Gertie hide
in the pumpkins.

"I want boots!" Ollie shouts.

Gossie and Gertie
stomp to Ollie.

Gossie gives Ollie a red boot.

Gertie gives Ollie a blue boot.

Ollie hops to the barn.

Gossie and Gertie follow.

Ollie stomps to the piggery.

Gossie and Gertie follow.

Ollie stares at his boots.

"These boots are too hot!"
Ollie shouts.

Ollie kicks off his boots.

Gossie kicks off her boot.
Gertie kicks off her boot.

"Let's go swimming!" Ollie shouts.
And they do.

Peedie

AGES	GRADES	GUIDED READING LEVEL	READING RECOVERY LEVEL	LEXILE® LEVEL
4–6	I	F	9–10	300L

This is Peedie.

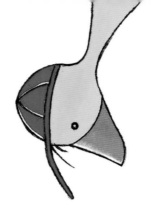

Peedie is a gosling.

A small, yellow gosling
who sometimes forgets things.

Peedie forgets things.
Even when Mama Goose
reminds him.

He forgets to come in
out of the rain.

He forgets to eat all his food.

He forgets to tidy his nest.

He forgets to take a nap.

He forgets to turn the egg.

But Peedie never forgets to
wear his lucky baseball cap.

He wears it everywhere
he goes.

He wears it when he dives.

He wears it when he slides.

He wears it when he explores.

He wears it when he snores.

Peedie never forgets to wear
his lucky red baseball cap.

Everywhere he goes.

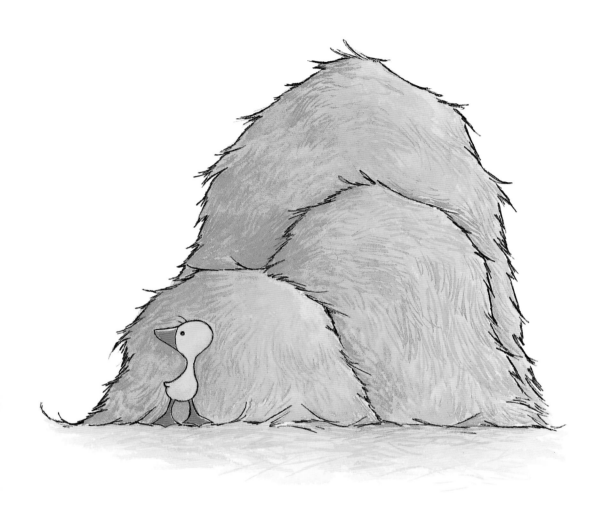

Then one day Peedie put
his lucky red baseball cap in
a secret place.

But he forgot where he put it.

He looked in the pond.

He looked in the apples.

He looked under the
flower pot.

He looked in the tall grass.

But Peedie could not
remember where he
had put it.

"Did you forget to turn the egg?" Mama Goose asked.

Peedie slowly trudged to the
nest. His lucky red baseball
cap was gone.

Then he saw it.
"There you are!" he said.

Peedie is a gosling.
A small, yellow gosling
who forgets things—
sometimes!

BooBoo

AGES	GRADES	GUIDED READING LEVEL	READING RECOVERY LEVEL	LEXILE® LEVEL
4–6	I	F	9–10	320L

This is BooBoo.

BooBoo is a gosling.

A small, blue gosling
who likes to eat.

BooBoo likes to eat from
morning till night.

Every day.

In the morning she eats
everything in her food bowl.

"Good food," she says.

BooBoo visits the hens
and gobbles their grain.

"Good food," she says.

BooBoo visits the goat
and pokes her bill into
the trough.

"Good food," she says.

BooBoo visits the mouse
and nibbles from his dish.

"Good food," she says.

Every afternoon BooBoo
goes for a swim in the pond.

She tastes the weeds.
"Good food," she says.

BooBoo is a curious
blue gosling.

Who likes to eat.

One afternoon BooBoo
saw bubbles floating
over the pond.

She opened her bill
and swallowed
a bright blue bubble.

"Good food," said BooBoo.

Then she burped.

She burped forward.

She burped backward.

She burped under water.

She burped in the weeds.

"Drink water!" said the turtle.
BooBoo guzzled and
gulped water.

She burped a teeny
tiny bubble.
"Good food," she said.

BooBoo is a gosling.
A small, blue gosling
who likes to eat.
Almost everything!

Gideon

AGES	GRADES	GUIDED READING LEVEL	READING RECOVERY LEVEL	LEXILE® LEVEL
4–6	1	E	7–8	260L

This is Gideon.

Gideon is a small, ruddy
gosling who likes to play.
All day.

Gideon marches
to the piggery.

He plays chase-the-piglet.

Gideon dashes
to the henhouse.

He plays find-the-eggs.

"Gideon, time for your nap,"
his mother calls.

"No nap! I'm playing!"

Gideon hops to the field.

He plays tag-the-mole.

Gideon chases butterflies
in the meadow.

He sneaks behind a beetle
on a rock.

"Gideon, time for your nap,"
his mother calls.

"No nap! I'm playing!"

Gideon scurries to the pond.

He splashes
with the ducklings.

Gideon scoots to the beehives.

He listens to the bees
buzzing inside the hive.

"Gideon, time for your nap,"
his mother calls.

"No nap! I'm playing!"

Gideon scampers
to the sheep house.

He bounces on the back
of the ewe.

Gideon leaps
over a green frog.

He plays quietly
with a small turtle.

Gideon wanders to the field.

He scrambles to the top
of the haystack.

"Gideon, time for your nap,"
his mother calls.

Gideon doesn't answer.

Gideon is a small, ruddy
gosling who likes to play . . .
almost all day.
Shhh . . .

Gideon & Otto

AGES	GRADES	GUIDED READING LEVEL	READING RECOVERY LEVEL	LEXILE® LEVEL
4–6	1	E	7–8	280L

This is Gideon.
Gideon is a small, ruddy gosling.

This is Otto.
Otto is Gideon's favorite friend.

Gideon carries Otto with him
everywhere he goes.

Otto likes to be carried.

Gideon swims with Otto.

Otto holds his breath.

Gideon hides with Otto.

Otto peeks out of the leaves.

Gideon reads to Otto.

Otto listens quietly.

Gideon sees two bunnies
playing.

He puts Otto on top of the
stone wall. "Stay here and
don't move," says Gideon.

Gideon dashes off to play.

Otto sits very still.
He quietly waits for Gideon.

Gideon and the bunnies leap
over a pumpkin.

"Catch me!" cries Gideon.

Gideon and the bunnies
scamper over the stone wall.

Otto tumbles into the grass.

"Gideon, time for dinner,"
Mama Goose calls.
The bunnies scurry home.

Gideon hops back to find Otto.
Otto is gone.

"Otto, time to go home,"
calls Gideon.

No Otto.

Gideon searches everywhere
for Otto.

But no Otto.

Gideon misses Otto.

Then he sees something
slowly moving in the grass.

"Otto!" shouts Gideon.

Otto rides on the back of
a green turtle.

Gideon loves Otto.
Otto loves Gideon.

Jasper&Joop

AGES	GRADES	GUIDED READING LEVEL	READING RECOVERY LEVEL	LEXILE® LEVEL
4–6	1	F	9–10	380L

This is Jasper.

This is Joop.

Jasper is a small, white gosling
who likes to be tidy.

Joop is a small, gray gosling
who likes to be messy.

Each morning Jasper tidies
his nest and puts on his cap
and tie.

Each morning Joop rumples
his nest and musses his
feathers.

Jasper pokes his head outside.
"It's wet," he says.

Joop pokes his head outside.
"It's WET!" he honks.

Jasper jumps over the puddle.
"Too wet," he says.

Joop splashes into the puddle.
"TOO wet!" he honks.

Jasper and Joop scurry to the piggery. "Come play!" squeal the piglets.

Jasper shakes his head.
Joop gleefully leaps into
the mud.

Jasper stares at Joop.
"Muddy mud," says Jasper.

Joop stares at Jasper.
"MUDDY mud!" honks Joop.

Jasper and Joop scamper to
the henhouse. "Come play!"
cheep the chicks.

Jasper shakes his head.
Joop rolls into the straw.

Jasper stares at Joop.
"Dusty straw," he says.

Joop stares at Jasper.
"DUSTY straw!" he honks.

Jasper and Joop scoot to
the beehive.
"Buzzzzzzzz!" warn the bees.

Jasper looks and listens.
Joop sticks his bill into
the beehive.

Jasper stares at Joop.
Joop stares at Jasper.

"RUN!" Jasper honks.

Jasper and Joop hide in the
grass. "RUN!" Jasper honks.

Jasper and Joop hide in the mud. "RUN!" Joop honks.

Jasper and Joop run to
the pond.

SPLASH!
Jasper and Joop jump into
the pond.

Jasper stares at Joop.
Joop stares at Jasper.

"What fun!" honk
Jasper and Joop.

Jasper laughs and flaps his
wings. Joop stands on a rock
and honks. They are best
friends.

Look for more Gossie&Friends®!

Gossie&Friends
A First Flap Book

Olivier Dunrea

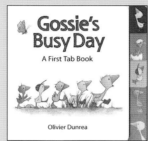

Gossie's Busy Day
A First Tab Book

Olivier Dunrea

Gossie Plays
HIDE and SEEK

Olivier Dunrea

Ollie's Easter Eggs

Olivier Dunrea
the creator of the best-selling Gossie&Friends books

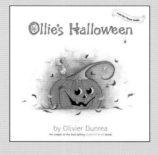

Ollie's Halloween

by Olivier Dunrea
the creator of the best-selling Gossie&Friends books

Merry Christmas, Ollie!

by Olivier Dunrea
the creator of the bestselling Gossie&Friends books

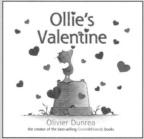

Ollie's Valentine

Olivier Dunrea
the creator of the best-selling Gossie&Friends books

www.hmhco.com

ISBN: 978-0-544-77980-8

Manufactured in China
SCP 10 9 8 7 6 5 4 3 2 1
4500615275